Published by
M A G I N A T I O N   P R E S S
An Educational Publishing Foundation Book
American Psychological Association
750 First Street, NE
Washington, DC 20002

For more information about our books, including a complete catalog, please write to us,
call 1-800-374-2721, or visit our website at www.maginationpress.com.

Editor: Darcie Conner Johnston
Art Director: Susan K. White
The text type is New Century Schoolbook
Printed by Phoenix Color, Rockaway, New Jersey

Library of Congress Cataloging-in-Publication Data

Sederman, Marty.
The magic box : when parents can't be there to tuck you in / written by Marty Sederman
and Seymour Epstein ; illustrated by Karen Stormer Brooks.
p. cm.
Summary: Casey and his father find a special way to share their love when his father
has to go away on business. Includes a note to caregivers.
ISBN 1-55798-807-2 (hc : alk. paper) — ISBN 1-55798-806-4 (pb : alk. paper)
[1. Father and son—Fiction. 2. Separation anxiety—Fiction.]
I. Epstein, Seymour. II. Brooks, Karen Stormer, ill. III. Title.
PZ7.S4479 Mag 2002
[E]—dc21   2002005458

Manufactured in the United States of America
10 9 8 7 6 5 4 3 2 1

The Magic Box

When Parents Can't Be There To Tuck You In

written by Marty Sederman and Seymour Epstein, Ph.D.
illustrated by Karen Stormer Brooks

MAGINATION PRESS • WASHINGTON, DC

To Casey and Derek — MS and SE

For Connor and Holly — KSB

Casey wore his favorite pajamas,
the red ones with polar bears playing soccer.

He washed up with his own bar of soap in
the shape of a sailboat.

He brushed his teeth with his panda bear
toothbrush.

"Time to pick out a story,"
called Mom.

Casey and Mom sat on the couch reading "Polar Pete's Arctic Adventure."

What was that? Casey's ears tingled. Was it the clump, clump, clump of footsteps and the jingle jangle of keys?

Yes! Daddy's home!

Casey rushed to the door and pounced on Dad.

"Can we play hide-and-seek, Dad? Can we?"

"The seeking champ is home!" said Dad.
"Tell you what, Case. You go hide in your
room while I say hi to Mom. I'll be there in
a few minutes."

Casey took off down the hall.

"Make me look really hard!" Dad called.

"You'll never find me!" shouted Casey.

From his secret spot, Casey could see Dad looking

under the bed...   under the the pillow...   in the drawers...
behind the curtains...   in the toy box...   under the rug...

Under the rug? Casey tried hard not to laugh.

"Oh-ho, I hear a mouse!" Dad cried and flung open the closet door.
"And there you are!"

"This time you hide," giggled Casey.

"No, it's bedtime now," said Dad. "Besides, I need time to think of a
really good hiding place."

"Tomorrow?" asked Casey, as he climbed into bed with his favorite bear, Ice Cap.

Dad put his arm around Casey. "I have to go away again for a couple of days. My plane leaves in the morning, but I'll be back on Friday, just in time for hide-and-seek."

"Oh no! Don't go!" pleaded Casey. **"Pleeeease?"**

"I wish I didn't have to," said Dad.

9

"It's not fair!" Casey wailed, throwing Ice Cap
on the floor. "John's father never goes away.
Why do YOU always go away?"

"Hey, Case," said Dad. "It's okay to be upset,
but let's not throw things. Ice Cap could get hurt."

"It just makes me mad that you have to go,"
Casey frowned.

"I know you feel mad—and sad too," said Dad.
"You know what? I miss you too when I'm gone."

"So why can't you stay home like John's dad?"

"John's dad and I do different things," Dad explained. "Sometimes I work with people who live far away, so I need to travel. Like your friend Whitney's mom. She's an airline pilot and travels a lot, too."

"But you're not a pilot. Why can't you just talk to people on the phone?" Casey asked.

"Sometimes I need to see people face to face," said Dad. "Like when you and John and Whitney built that huge city out of blocks."

Casey thought for a minute. "Yeah," he said, "we couldn't do that on the phone. We had to be together."

"You know what else, Casey? When I'm away,
I try to picture how great it will be when I see you
and Mom again, and I think about what we can all
do together when I get home."

Casey's face lit up. "Hey, why don't I think of something
we can all do together when you get home?"

"Great idea!" Dad kissed Casey in the middle of his
forehead and patted Ice Cap goodnight. "Sleep tight,"
he whispered.

Casey started making plans. "First we'll fix pancakes for Mom. Then I'll show Dad that I can ride my bike without training wheels. Then we can all ride to the park and hunt for butterflies and frogs. Then we can stop for ice cream, and I'll get a chocolate cone with sprinkles. And when we get home, we'll build a block tower up to the ceiling and play hide and seek. Then ... "

"It's Thursday," said Mom the next morning as she flipped French toast. "Don't you do news today at school?"

"I'm going to tell all the kids and Ms. Bifano that I can ride my bike without training wheels," said Casey. "And that Dad doesn't know, and that I'm going to surprise him this weekend."

"Good morning, all you sunny faces," said Ms. Bifano. "It's time for weekly news. Shall we form a circle?"

Casey stashed his polar bear lunch box in his cubby.

John scrunched closer to Whitney to make a spot for him.

"So who has news to share?" Ms. Bifano looked around the circle and wiggled her eyebrows for fun.

John's hand shot up. "My grandparents are here for a whole week. They came all the way from California!"

"Lucky you, John!" said Ms. Bifano. "Whitney?"

"That's so funny because my mom just went to California last night. She's a pilot, you know."

"I wonder where Dad is this time," thought Casey, as he waved his hand in the air.

"Where's Dad this time?"
Casey asked Mom after school.

"He's in Montreal," she said. "That's a city in Canada.
Would you like to find it on the map?"

Casey pulled out his giant "Atlas of the World"
and flipped through the maps with Mom.

"Here's Canada," she said, "and here's Montreal,
where this little star is."

"And here's where we live," said Casey, pointing to
an orange shape and tracing a line with his finger
to Montreal.

"When I grow up," said Casey, "I'm not going to travel. I'm not even going to work. I'm going to play with my kids all day."

"Your kids are going to be very lucky," said Mom. "Most parents have to work to pay for things like their house and food and toys."

"But when I grow up," Casey said, "just the mom can work."

Mom looked into Casey's face. "Are you missing Dad?"

Casey started to shake his head no, and then changed his mind. "I guess so," he nodded.

"Wait right here," said Mom, ducking out of the room. She came back carrying a glittery box covered with deep purple paper and gold stars. On the top, in silver letters, the box said CASEY.

"Dad made this for you."

Casey bounced up and down. "What is it? What's inside?"

"He left a note," answered Mom. "It says…"

Dear Casey —
This is a magic box. I put some hugs and kisses in it for you, so you will know how much I love you even when I'm away. There is a surprise in the box, too. I can't wait to see you tomorrow and find out what you've planned for this weekend.

Love, Dad

Casey reached for the box, but Mom held it high over his head.

"Mom!" Casey laughed, "I want to see!"

"I know," said Mom grinning, "but Dad said I have to deliver his hugs and kisses first."

She opened the box a crack and slid her hand inside. "Got 'em!"

Mom wrapped her arms around Casey and kissed
him squarely on the forehead, just like Dad always
did. Casey shut his eyes and imagined his father.

"Dad loves you very much," whispered Mom,
"and so do I. Now here's your magic box."

Casey lifted the lid. In the box, taped to one side, was a picture of Dad and Casey. On the other side Dad had colored a big red heart. And lying on the bottom was a new set of markers.

"Markers!" Casey exclaimed. "I'm going to make something for Dad, something

really special!

"Can I use this?"
Casey asked his mom the next day.

He held up a small white box.

"Sure," said Mom. "What for?"

"I'm going to make a magic box for Dad so he can
have MY hugs and kisses when he's away," said Casey.
"It's little, so it can fit in his suitcase."

"Great idea!" said Mom.

Casey gathered up his sticker
collection, some paper, a glue stick,
and his new markers.

He set them on the table with the little white
box, and pulled up an extra chair for Ice Cap.

"First I'll draw a picture of me and Dad and paste
it in the bottom," he explained to Ice Cap. "Then
I'll make a big heart on the lid. And then we'll
put some of these really cool stickers all over it."

"Now for the most important part," he said.

1 2 3 4

Casey blew four kisses into the box.
He squeezed himself in a big bear hug and slipped the hug into the box.

Quickly, he pressed the lid over the top so that nothing could escape,
and held up the box for Ice Cap to admire.

"TA-DA! I hope Dad likes it!"

"Time for dinner,"
called Mom.

After dinner, Casey donned his second-favorite pair of pajamas, the blue ones with penguins playing hockey.

He washed up with his own bar of soap in the shape of a sailboat.

He brushed his teeth with his panda bear toothbrush.

"Time to pick out a story,"

called Mom.

Casey and Mom sat on the couch reading "Stewart Squirrel Saves the Day." What was that? Casey's ears tingled.

The clump, clump, clump of footsteps?

The jingle jangle of keys?

Yes! Daddy's home!

Casey rushed to the door...

…and pounced on Dad in the doorway.

"Look, Dad! I made a magic box for you, too!
I already put in kisses and a big hug, so don't
open it until you go away next time, okay?"

"Wow!" said Dad. "This is great, Casey.
I promise not to peek."

"And I thought of all kinds of fun things to
do this weekend. Do you want to hear?"

"Tell you what," said Dad. "I'm going to
say hi to Mom for a few minutes.
Then I'll tuck you in, and you can tell me
all about everything."

 Casey kissed Mom goodnight and dashed down the hall.

"I hope your plans include some hide-and-seek," Dad called, "because I've got a really, really good hiding place in mind. You'll never find me."

"No way!" shouted Casey. "I'll find you! I always do!"

Note to Parents

BY ANN RASMUSSEN, PSY.D.

Today's children often face short separations from their parents because of far-flung work demands or family commitments. In the common chaos of family life, their reactions to parental comings and goings may be overlooked. But when parents travel, feelings usually do arise in children that are difficult for young minds to understand and express—feelings that include fear, rejection, anger, helplessness, sadness, and loneliness.

Such feelings are normal and expectable. Indeed, children have such troubling feelings precisely because they love and need their parents so much. On the positive side, the brief absence of a loved one is a vital learning opportunity for children, who will inevitably suffer disruptions of their closest relationships throughout life. Where better to struggle with and learn to manage difficult feelings than in the safe, small circle of the family?

Like adults, children fare better when they can take an active role in navigating disappointing situations, rather than passively putting up with unwanted events. Children are best helped toward this end when their parents can be their partners and coaches. Accepting the child's difficult feelings, guiding the child in identifying those feelings, and responding with a creative problem-solving attitude help the child acquire emotional skills and maturity, especially when the difficult feelings are in relation to the parents themselves.

The Magic Box suggests several techniques that parents can follow to help their children prepare for absences and bridge the gulf while the parent is away.

◉ Inform children about a trip beforehand. Whenever possible, the traveling parent should deliver the news. Give the child some advance notice, such as the day or evening before the trip, and choose both a time and a place that allow for an open, unhurried discussion. Surprise absences breed insecurity in young children as well as heightened feelings of anger and sadness.

◉ Talk openly about the child's feelings, including those feelings that children fear their parents won't like, such as anger at being left, frustration, disappointment, and sadness. If the child expresses these hard feelings (or tries not to!), help him or her identify the feelings by name, and offer reassurance that such feelings are normal. In this way, the child gets "permission" to have these feelings, and can so begin to work through them more consciously and constructively.

❊ For the parent who remains at home or another caregiver, try to be aware of the child's feelings while the traveling parent is away, and continue to talk about them. Consider the possibility that irritability, grouchiness, and being "out of sorts" may be due to the child's missing the absent parent.

◉ Talk about the reunion and make plans for that time, so that the absence doesn't seem interminable. This makes the return more concrete for the child by giving him or her something specific to think about and look forward to. Also, when children can make plans in this way, they feel more control over the situation, and less powerless.

★ Help the child visualize where the parent will be, using maps and other resources. A trip to the library, a session on the Internet, and a look at an encyclopedia or travel guide are other fun ways a child may investigate the parent's destination and feel connected. Parent and child can talk about what the child has discovered when the parent returns.

◉ Make a magic box as a kind of portable connection device, wherein loving notes, photos, jokes, and so forth can be left for enjoyment in each other's absence as a substitute for actual contact.

Here are additional strategies that parents can use to help bridge the gap of travel distance between themselves and their children:

Make or buy a calendar. Write in activities and special events that will fill the days during the parent's absence, such as a trip to the zoo, a play date, an after-school class, team practice, or a friend's birthday party. Also, mark the parent's return date on the calendar. Check the days off at bedtime, so that the child can see that the parent's return is getting closer. If a child is too young to comprehend calendar time, use a string and clothespins or paperclips to represent the days until the parent's return, removing a marker at the end of each day.

The traveling parent can make a "Mommy tape" or "Daddy tape" that might include favorite bedtime stories being read to the child, favorite songs, things they look forward to doing upon their return, funny memories, or things they love about the child. Perhaps it is overkill, but the parent can do the same on videotape. Such a video might be nice to have for posterity, in any case!

While the traveling parent is away, help the child make an audiotape diary of daily events and funny or interesting occurrences for the parent to listen to upon return.

Children can also make a picture diary of each day while the parent is absent.

Leave notes or goofy pictures to be delivered or discovered each night during the absence.

Send emails back and forth between parent and child.

Call the child regularly. If the child is out or asleep, and you have an answering machine, leave a lengthy, loving, positive message.

Take a small toy or stuffed animal of your child's on the trip to care for as a substitute for the child. Younger children especially delight in this notion. Traveling parents can offer something of their own in turn, such as a special photo of the parent and child together, a scarf, a tie, a baseball mitt, and so on.

Invite the child to have an important job that links him or her with the parent during the absence. For example, the child can water newly planted flowers or watch out for favorite sport team scores.

All of the above activities teach children that although a loved one is physically absent, he or she can still be connected with in many loving ways. Children are thus helped to develop a greater sense of love's endurance and their own mastery of helpless feelings, using active communication and reaching-out strategies. In the meantime, parents should rest assured (and not allow insidious guilt to creep in) that short leave-takings can be positive, growth-promoting experiences for children. The key is to approach children as their nonjudgmental, understanding, strategizing partners.

Ann Rasmussen, Psy.D., is a clinical psychologist, therapist, and author of The Very Lonely Bathtub. *She lives in New Jersey with her husband and three children.*

About the Authors

MARTY SEDERMAN came up with the idea of a "magic box" to help her children while their dad was away on frequent business trips — and it worked so well that she decided to write a book about it. A market research consultant, Ms. Sederman holds an M.B.A. from Harvard Business School and a master's degree in clinical psychology. She lives in New Jersey with her family.

SEYMOUR EPSTEIN, PH.D., is Marty Sederman's father. Dr. Epstein, professor emeritus of psychology at the University of Massachusetts, has a doctoral degree in adult and child clinical psychology. He has published extensively in professional journals and is the author of several books, including *Constructive Thinking: The Key to Emotional Intelligence*.

About the Illustrator

KAREN STORMER BROOKS is the illustrator of several children's books, including *Elana's Ears* by Gloria Roth Lowell and *Dylan, the Eagle-Hearted Chicken* by David L. Harrison. Her illustrations have appeared in many children's publications, such as *Highlights for Children*, *Spider*, and *Cricket* magazines. She lives with her family in Atlanta, Georgia.